DO NOT REMOVE
CARDS FROM POCKET

For Brenda   C.T.

Text copyright © 1994 by Kathy Henderson
Illustrations copyright © 1994 by Carol Thompson

First U.S. edition 1994
Published in Great Britain in 1994 by Walker Books Ltd., London.

Library of Congress Cataloging-in-Publication Data

Henderson, Kathy, 1949–
Bumpety bump / Kathy Henderson ; illustrated by Carol Thompson.—
1st U.S. ed.
Summary: As she's passed from one family member to
another, Baby enjoys a rollicking ride.
ISBN 1-56402-312-5
[1. Babies—Fiction.   2. Family life—Fiction.   3. Stories in rhyme.]
I. Thompson, Carol, ill.   II. Title.
PZ8.3.H4144Bu   1994
[E]—dc20   93-3541

10 9 8 7 6 5 4 3 2 1

Printed in Italy

The pictures in this book were done in watercolor and ink.

Candlewick Press
2067 Massachusetts Avenue
Cambridge, Massachusetts 02140

Bumpety Bump

Kathy Henderson
illustrated by Carol Thompson

CANDLEWICK PRESS
CAMBRIDGE, MASSACHUSETTS

The baby went
for a ride,

a-bumpety-bumpety-bump!

She rode in her
sister's arms,

a-slumpety-slumpety-slump!

She rode on her
grandpa's knee,

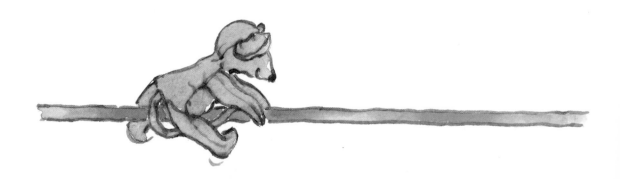

a-tumpety-tumpety-tump!

She rode on her
mother's hip,

a-lumpety-lumpety-lump!

She rode on her
uncle's neck,

a-humpety-humpety-hump!

And flew high
up in the air,

a-jumpety-jumpety-jump!

She rode around
and about
and then...

went back to
sleep in her
crib again.